Strawberry Shortcake
Plays Soccer

Grosset & Dunlap

Library of Congress Cataloging-in-Publication Data is available.

ISBN 0-448-43207-2   A B C D E F G H I J

Special Markets ISBN 0-448-43709-0

Strawberry Shortcake
Plays Soccer

By Ruth Koeppel
Illustrated by Ken Edwards

Grosset & Dunlap • New York

"Strawberry, you're late! You promised you would practice soccer drills with me today," Huck said.

"I'm sorry, Huck," said Strawberry Shortcake. "But as I was walking through Cookie Corners I met Ginger Snap. And

then Angel Cake joined us at Cakewalk. And in Orange Blossom Acres we picked up Orange Blossom…"

"Maybe this isn't a bad thing after all," said Huck. "Now we can have a real practice. There's enough of us for a game!"

"Come on, everyone," Huck called out.
"Let's head to the clubhouse!"
     "Don't athletes usually have big breakfasts?"
Angel Cake grumbled. "I didn't eat before we left."

Ginger Snap laughed. "Don't worry.
We'll have a snack before we start playing,"
she said, pointing at her knapsack.

Angel Cake groaned as she put on a pair of soccer shoes with cleats. "Why can't we just wear our sneakers?" she asked.

"Because the cleats grip the ground. You can run on the field better in cleats than in sneakers," Huck told her.

Strawberry Shortcake and Huckleberry gathered up gear.
"It's also important to wear safety gear. We don't want anybody to
get hurt," said Ginger Snap, sneaking Angel Cake a handful of cookies.

"Let's start with some drills," said Huck. "Just like we do in real soccer practice."

"Hold on a second," said Angel. "I think we should start with warm-ups. Okay, everybody, stretch!" Angel Cake bent down and grabbed her ankles.

"Can't we just start the game already?"
Ginger Snap burst out.

"Time out!" Strawberry told her friends.
"Angel Cake's right, we should warm up.
Let's jog in a circle!"

"Okay, enough jogging," Huck decided, coming to a sudden stop.

Strawberry Shortcake ran right into him. Huck fell, and Strawberry landed on top of him. Angel Cake landed on Strawberry. Ginger Snap topped off the group.

"Let's practice some passes," came Huck's muffled voice.

Strawberry practiced a
throw-in from the sidelines. Huck
kicked it back to her.

"Heads up!" he called out as the ball
whizzed toward Strawberry.

"Hats down!" she sighed as the ball knocked her hat off.

Angel showed everyone the right way to kick the ball.

"When you shoot, kick the ball with the front of your shoe," she told her friends.

Everyone started to practice kicking. Then, with a giant plunk, Huck fell on his rear end.

Angel Cake giggled.

"Are you okay?" asked Strawberry Shortcake, kneeling by Huck's side.

"You bet," Huck said, jumping up. "Let's pick teams!"

"Strawberry and I will be the team captains," announced Huck.
"But I want to be a captain," Angel Cake cried.
"That's fine with me," Strawberry Shortcake said quickly.
Huck shrugged, and flipped a gingersnap high in the air.

"Tops-up, Angel Cake picks first," he said. "Bottoms-up, I start."

The cookie landed tops-up. Angel Cake picked Ginger Snap.

"Why didn't you pick me?" asked Strawberry Shortcake. "I thought we were best friends."

"I choose Strawberry," Huck said.

"Orange Blossom, come join my team," called Angel Cake.

"Whatever team I play on, it will be uneven. We can't have a fair game with three against two," said Orange Blossom.

Just then, Honey Pie Pony galloped over. "How about I play? That will even things out."

"That's a great idea, Honey," said Strawberry. "Hey, it looks like Custard and Pupcake want to play, too!"

"Okay, so it's Strawberry, Honey Pie, Custard, and me on one team, and Angel Cake, Ginger Snap, Orange Blossom, and Pupcake on the other," said Huck.

"Let's play ball!" said Angel Cake.

The game began. Angel Cake dribbled the ball away from Huck and traveled down the field toward Strawberry Shortcake's goal. But Huck gave the ball a swift kick and sent it far out of Angel Cake's reach.

"I've got it, Huck!" cried Honey Pie, clamping down on the ball with her front hoof.

Angel Cake raced toward Honey Pie. But the pony passed the ball back to Huck, who set off with it down the field.

Huck kicked the ball hard, and it sped past Orange Blossom and Ginger Snap, into the net.

"He shoots...he scores!" Huck cried.

Ginger Snap picked up the ball and threw it out of the goal.

"Time out!" Angel Cake called. "No one on my team is paying attention!"

Pupcake growled.

"Sorry, Angel," said Orange Blossom. "Ginger was just telling me..."

"Come on, guys," Angel interrupted. "Let's play soccer! We can chat later."

Angel Cake zoomed forward and knocked the ball away from Huck. Huck chased Angel Cake down the field. Angel Cake ran all the way to Strawberry Shortcake's goal. Strawberry was reaching for the ball when Angel kicked it—hard!

"Ouch!" cried Strawberry.

"Oh, Strawberry, I'm so sorry," Angel Cake cried.

"It's okay," Strawberry Shortcake said softly.

"Angel, what's the point of playing if you're going to be a bad sport?" Huck asked, running over to help Strawberry Shortcake.

"Huck's right," said Angel. "I wanted to win so badly that I didn't think about anyone's feelings."

Angel Cake went over to Ginger Snap.
"Do you want to switch positions, Ginger?"
Angel Cake asked. "You can be
forward now," she added.

At that moment, Apple Dumplin' crawled by.
She rolled the ball through the goal posts,
right past Strawberry Shortcake.

Strawberry Shortcake picked up Apple Dumplin'.
"You did it, sweetie," she said. "You scored a goal!"
"That makes it a tied score!" Huck said. "I say we
go back to my fort for some huckleberry pie!"
Everyone cheered.

"Strawberry, I'm sorry about hurting you before. Our friendship is so much more important than a silly old soccer game," said Angel Cake.